CAPTAIN COSMIC PICKLE

written by Carmellia Watson

illustrated by Katerina Valerieva

Text © 2024 by Carmellia Watson. All rights reserved. No part of this publication may be reproduced or transmitted in any form or by any means, electronic or mechanical, including photocopy, recording, or any information storage and retrieval system, without permission in writing from the copyright owner.

Illustrations © 2024 by Beytler Illustrations.

Dedicated to:

I dedicate this book to my mother Bertha, my husband Joe, my children Carrisa, Jonathan, and Cullen, my grandchildren Harmonee, Jonathan Jr., Rome, Carrina, and Cordale, my brother Nathan, my sister Roberta (whom I lost in June 2024), my sister Glenda, my sister-in-law Annettia Watson, Bonita Mullins, and the church family at the Center of Hope. My biggest fans are Brenda, Bethany, Angelise, Norma, Michelle-P, Yadira, and Maura. Special thanks to Katerina for the amazing illustrations. I would also like to recognize Jason and Dwayne, my Godbrothers, and Amanda, my Godsister, for their support. Thanks for making this book possible.

About the Author

Carmellia Watson aka "Car" was born and raised in Reno Nevada. She is a mother of three and a grandmother of five. What is a Queen without a King; her King's name is Joe. She enjoys hearing young inventive minds share stories and songs written by them.

She enjoys writing for young minds and enticing them to color and write outside the box and boundaries of this world. Her characters are relatable to children and adults making reading fun and exciting. The power of imagination is what keeps us young.

Foreword
by Robert Graham

It is with great enthusiasm that I write the foreword for this delightful and imaginative book. Within these pages, Carmellia Watson has crafted a story that is as colorful and vibrant as the communities of Blueberry and Broccoli Ville themselves. This tale of friendship, collaboration, and resilience brings to life the magic of unity and the power of creativity in solving even the most puzzling mysteries.

From the moment I was introduced to the unique mayors and the intriguing mystery that grips these two enchanting cities, I was captivated. Through vivid descriptions and heartfelt storytelling, the world of Blueberry and Broccoli Ville springs to life, inviting readers of all ages to step into a realm where kindness and teamwork triumph.

Carmellia's work is not just a story—it is a celebration of the values that hold us together as families, communities, and friends. Whether you are young or young at heart, this book will leave you smiling, inspired, and perhaps even craving a slice of the famous blueberry broccoli pie!

As you journey through these pages, I invite you to embrace the lessons within: that challenges are best met with collaboration, that everyone—no matter how small—has a voice that matters, and that heroes can be found in the most unexpected places.

Congratulations to Carmellia Watson on a tale well told, and to you, dear reader, for embarking on this wonderful adventure. Enjoy the magic.

With admiration,
Robert Graham

Once upon a time, there were two cities. One was called Blueberry, and the other city was called Broccoli Ville. Both cities were full of color. The roads were bright orange with a touch of brown. The sky was light blue with a pinch of white and a trace of yellow. All the houses in the neighborhood were filled with beauty and bright colors everywhere. The front and back yards were big, with a lot of green grass. The trees were tall, with branches so big and strong, full of leaves. At night, the sky was a darker shade of blue and full of yellow, dancing stars. The moon lit up the sky with a laughing smile.

Let us talk about the beautiful weather. It was always sunny and warm during the day. Of course, there were a few months when it rained. Some days, it felt like the rain would go on and on, never stopping.

The cities needed the rain because it kept everything so green and bright. The people of these cities had never seen snow, and the temperature was never below 60 degrees.

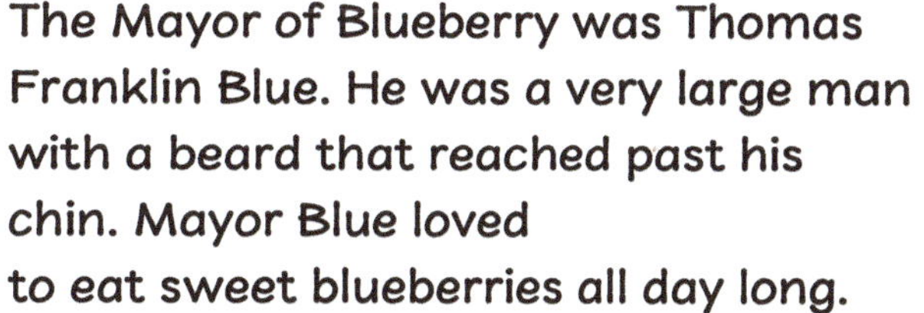

The Mayor of Blueberry was Thomas Franklin Blue. He was a very large man with a beard that reached past his chin. Mayor Blue loved to eat sweet blueberries all day long.

The Mayor of Broccoli Ville was Theodore Stanley Green. He was the opposite of Mayor Blue. Mayor Green was short, with red hair that looked like fire blowing in the wind. He loved to eat broccoli all day. Both mayors were very nice and good with people, and they enjoyed making sure their cities were safe and happy.

Broccoli Ville and Blueberry were great places to live. The adults worked gathering fruit in Blueberry and vegetables in Broccoli Ville. The children went to school to learn about everything, and when they got home, they enjoyed life in the sun.

Life in both places was great, and everyone got along with each other.

One summer day, Mayor Green of Broccoli Ville got a call from Mayor Blue of Blueberry, saying something very strange was going on.

Someone was going around stealing all the blueberries, strawberries, grapes, and oranges from the yards and along the main street. It was a big mystery.
He and his staff could not find who or what was doing this.
Wow!! Crime in Blueberry was unheard of.

The city of Blueberry made lots of money by selling its sweet-tasting fruit.
They could sell their fruit not only to local stores but also to surrounding areas, including Broccoli Ville.

This was a big deal, and the thief had to be stopped. If the mystery was not solved soon, the people of Blueberry would not be able to pay their bills.
What would they do if they couldn't find out what was going on? One thing was for sure—something had to be done right away.

Mayor Blue and the people of Blueberry gathered for a meeting to decide what they should do about this problem.

One farmer said, "We should stay awake all night and watch the city like an eagle."

A small voice in the middle of the room came from a small boy standing behind a very tall man. The boy said, "Why don't we put up cameras around the city, and some of them in the yards up in the trees? Then, in the morning, we could see what the cameras recorded."

The mayor said, "That is a great idea!"
The men of Blueberry put up cameras along the main street and in the front and back of some yards throughout the neighborhood.

Late that night, when all of Blueberry was sleeping in their soft, warm beds, two shadows appeared, lurking around the neighborhood.
They were looking for the best fruit to steal from the yards and the streets.

The shadows did not see the cameras that were hidden, so they went on about their business. Grabbing strawberries, blueberries, peaches, oranges, cherries, and apples off the tall trees, they also took some ripe grapes. The bag was big, full, and heavy. It took both of them to carry it away.

The next day, Mayor Blue and the men of Blueberry got up to watch what was recorded on the cameras. To everyone's surprise, they could only see shadows. They could not see who or what the shadows were.

One shadow was tall and thin but had something on its head. The other one was also tall and thin, but it was still a mystery why they were stealing the fruit. Not wasting any time, the mayor called for help from Mayor Green of Broccoli Ville.

"Mayor Green, I really need your help with this case. Is there anyone you can send to Blueberry?"

The Mayor of Broccoli Ville said, "Of course, Mayor Blue. My men and I will be there as soon as we can."

Mayor Green of Broccoli Ville gathered his men and told them that Blueberry needed their help to catch the mysterious shadows that were going around stealing fruit. All the men of Broccoli Ville were surprised, having never heard of crime in their city. The men wanted to help. They all started shouting, "We'll do it, Mayor! We'll catch those shadow thieves!"

"All right, then. We will head out in the morning," said Mayor Green. The men arrived after a long day's trip but were still excited about catching the shadow thieves that night. Mayor Blue was so happy to see so many people come to help.

"All right, Mayor Blue, what's the plan, and what do you need us to do?"
yelled a man from the back corner.

"The first order of business is to get you men fed," said Mayor Blue.

"Sounds good to me," said Mayor Green.

Mayor Blue said, "Come on down to the park. The fine ladies of Blueberry
have cooked a feast fit for a king."

Mayor Green and the men followed Mayor Blue down to the park. Everyone's
eyes widened, and their faces lit up with joy from the wonderful smells
coming from the park.

The tables were full of food. There was fried chicken, pot roast, dinner rolls,
potato salad, baked beans, and desserts to die for— apple, cherry, blueberry,
and strawberry pies, chocolate cake, brownies, cookies of all kinds, and yes,
ice cream. They sat around eating, laughing, making jokes, and telling stories.

The children played volleyball, basketball, and baseball in the open field. It was
a wonderful day.

Mayor Blue got up from the table to make a speech. Clearing his throat, he said, "Um! Oh! I am indeed happy that our good friends from Broccoli Ville have come to help us solve this crime. I want everyone to be on the lookout, and we will keep the cameras up as backup. We don't know what we are dealing with, so be careful."

As soon as he finished talking, the kids went back to playing, and laughter once again filled the park.

Later that night, the cameras were on, and the men were waiting outside, hiding on the streets and in the backyards of some houses in the neighborhood. The night was quiet and still—you could only hear the crickets singing in the cool night wind. But wait! There was a noise coming from down the street, around the corner, next to the trash can behind the house on the left. Some of the men started to tiptoe toward the sound. They heard whispers when suddenly two shadows flew by them, knocking over one of the men.

"Wow!! What was that? Who was that?" said one of the men standing near the trash can. "Come on, let me help you up, young lad."

"Somebody, go and get Mayor Blue!" Mayor Blue came running down the street. "Great blue and orange smokes! Are you all right?" the mayor said. "It happened so fast, it was hard to see anything."

"Come on, let's see what the cameras recorded." The men and both mayors gathered at Mayor Blue's house to watch. Once again, the only thing visible was two shadows.

Both were tall and thin, with something on the head of one. "We have a real mystery here. We might need to call on a hero," said Mayor Blue. "There's a rumor that a hero, known as Captain Cosmic Pickle, lives somewhere between the two cities. Nobody really knows for sure. They only know that he stands for justice and peace."
"How will we reach or get hold of this hero?" asked one of the men. "Good question," Mayor Blue said. "I heard he likes blueberry broccoli pie."

"What?! Blueberry broccoli pie?" exclaimed Mayor Green. "That's right—the best of both towns. Mayor Green, get your wife here, and along with my wife, they will work together making the pie."
"Okay," Mayor Green said. "I hope it works."

No one had ever heard of such a pie. Some of the people thought the mayor had lost his mind. The idea of a fruity vegetable pie did not sound good at all. The other question was: how did Mayor Blue hear about a hero named "Cosmic Pickle"?

The women got together, though they didn't have a recipe for such a pie. Mayor Blue's wife said, "I'll get the fattest, juiciest, sweetest blueberries for my pie." Mayor Green's wife said, "Well, I'll get the roundest, plumpest, greenest broccoli for mine." Who would have thought to put the two together?

The women got into the kitchen and started making the crust for the pie. Then, they put the filling together, using blueberries, broccoli, flour, butter, cornstarch, and a little sugar. The pie went into the oven to bake for about an hour. Once it was done, they set it outside on a table, hoping that the smell of the pie would bring the hero.

As time went by, it seemed as if no one would come. All the men, women, and children waited outside, looking around. "Look! It's a funny-looking bird in the sky!"

"No, it's a small plane!" "No! I think it's Captain Cosmic Pickle!" The flying object landed right by the pie, smelling it as if it was the best thing ever— better than toys and ice cream. "Is this pie for me?" said the pickle. All the people stood there, mouths open, not sure what they were looking at. Mayor Blue said, "Yes, it is, but we need your help." The pickle stood there, wearing a yellow cape around his neck and a black fedora hat on his head. He had the most beautiful white teeth they had ever seen, with a big smile on his face. "What can I do for you, dear mayor?" he asked after picking up the pie.

Mayor Blue said, "We caught mysterious shadows stealing our fruit from the yards throughout the neighborhood and along the main streets. This is how we make our living."

"Shadows, you say, dear mayor?"

"Yes, shadows—two of them. They only come out at night while we are sleeping."

"I will help you catch these thieves tonight." It took a while for the sky to turn dark. Just as soon as it did, the hero told the men to be ready and keep their eyes open. There was a huge blueberry bush on Main Street, ready for harvest. This was where Captain Cosmic Pickle hid. The two shadows, trying not to make any noise, crept closer and closer to the bush. Just as they reached for the bush, Captain Cosmic Pickle jumped out and squirted slimy green pickle juice on the ground.

The two shadows slipped and fell to the ground, and the men threw nets over them. Everyone started cheering. "You got them! You got them! This is a great night for Blueberry!"

"Now let's see who they are." Captain Cosmic Pickle pulled off their black suits, revealing their faces. It was Mr. Carrot and Mrs. Phoebe String Bean! "These two thieves are wanted in several other cities," said the captain. "They have committed a string of crimes throughout the country."

"How can we ever thank you, Captain Cosmic Pickle?" asked Mayor Blue. "More pie, please!" the hero replied with a grin. Just before he flew away, he told the people, "Whenever you need me, I will always be a pie away."

The good people of Blueberry and Broccoli Ville celebrated together.

THE END